THE ADVENTURES OF
ODD AND ELSEWHERE

James Roose-Evans

One morning a small bear called Odd wakes up to
see the removal van drive away. 'The odds are,'
he murmurs to himself, 'that I am the only
person left in this house, and what could be
odder than that?' But he soon has very odd
company indeed when he finds a circus clown
called Elsewhere hanging upside-down in a
cupboard. The two friends decide to team up and
go and live in Fenton House, next door, together
with Collander Moll, the caretaker, and her father
Hallelujah Jones, a retired Welsh policeman who
does the garden. This is just the start of Odd and
Elsewhere's extraordinary adventures together.

THE ADVENTURES OF

ODD &
ELSEWHERE

BY JAMES ROOSE-EVANS

WITH PICTURES BY BRIAN ROBB

A Magnet Book

Also in Magnet books by the same author:

THE SECRET OF THE SEVEN BRIGHT SHINERS
ODD AND THE GREAT BEAR
ELSEWHERE AND THE CLOWNS

Other books about Odd and Elsewhere are:

THE RETURN OF THE GREAT BEAR
THE SECRET OF TIPPITY WITCHET
THE LOST TREASURE OF WALES

Published by André Deutsch

First published in Great Britain 1972
by André Deutsch Ltd, 105 Great Russell Street,
London WC1
Magnet paperback edition published 1981
by Methuen Children's Books Ltd,
11 New Fetter Lane, London EC4P 4EE
Reprinted 1982
Copyright © 1972 by James Roose-Evans
Drawings © 1972 by Brian Robb
All rights reserved
Printed in Great Britain by
Richard Clay (The Chaucer Press) Ltd,
Bungay, Suffolk

ISBN 0 416 24300 2

For ELEANOR FARJEON
in gratitude for so many hours
of friendship in Hampstead

Fenton House in Hampstead, London, belongs to the National Trust, and is open to the public. The National Trust, which was founded in 1894, helps to save and preserve the nation's historic houses, castles, gardens and thousands of acres of land that might otherwise be lost or destroyed.

ONE

Sprawled in a corner, the small bear could see the removal van drive away. Everybody had gone and he was left alone in the empty house. He was feeling extra sorry for himself because he had also caught a cold. For as long as he had known Odd had never had any trousers, only a blue and white striped shirt which, by dint of tugging, he had managed to stretch into a skirt or kilt – but still he felt very draughty.

He could hear old Hallelujah in the garden next door rattling his wheelbarrow down the path. The early morning sun shone warmly in at the window and for a while he just lay there. Then he sneezed sharply in the dust and got up to explore.

'The odds are,' he murmured to himself, 'that I am the only person left in this house, and what could be odder than that?' He paused for a moment, cocking his head towards a reflection of himself, encountered that moment in a piece of broken mirror tilted against the wall.

'Indeed,' he murmured sagely to his reflected self, 'what could be odder than Odd?'

'Or who?' came a voice at that moment.

Odd looked around the empty room. He felt like saying, 'Is there anybody there?' but decided this might sound a little odd.

'Dedadedadedadeda!' he sang tunelessly, unable to make up his mind.

'Odds and boddikins!' exclaimed the voice, 'is that supposed to be an ode or an oddity? Come and help me get out of here!'

The sing-song voice seemed to come from inside a tall cupboard. Knotting together the tail ends of his shirt, Odd ambled over to contemplate the problem of opening a cupboard, the handle of which was too high for him to reach.

'If you pull and I push, you'll find the door is only stuck,' said the voice.

'Ah, but don't you see,' explained Odd, 'except that you can't see – of course, I see that – that I'm too short to reach the handle. Now, let me see!'

All these 'sees' were beginning to make him see-sick, so he put his paws behind his back and began to pace up and down. Suddenly he noticed the flex of the electric light hanging from one wall.

Taking hold of the switch he walked backwards and took a running jump at the cupboard. If only he could catch hold of the door handle as he flew past . . .

Crash! bang! ouch! Odd lay on the floor battered and bruised.

'Odds boddikins!' screamed the voice within, 'there's no need to batter in the door!'

Odd took a deep breath, counted up to twenty, and then said with icy dignity, 'I shall try again and will you please forbear from comment. Otherwise I shall not bother to assist you. I have a great deal to do and far more important things than listening to strange voices in strange cupboards!'

Once more he took hold of the long flex and after several tries succeeded in swinging up to the handle and holding on to it. There was a pause while he hung there, wondering what next to do. From the other side of the cupboard came soft bumps.

'Pull, can't you!' said the voice rather peevishly.

'I can't!' replied Odd, his arms beginning to ache and

his paws starting to slip. Once again he fell to the floor, this time landing on the lump made by his shirt tails knotted together.

'Ouch!' he cried.

'Oh, for Odd's sake!' screamed the voice, rising to a malevolent shriek of exasperation. 'What *are* you doing?'

It was at this moment that Odd's nose started to become unstitched, and he sat there, feeling distinctly sorry for himself and very much at odds with the world, staring cross-eyed at his running nose.

The long flex, weighted by the switch at the end, swung back and forth, like the tail of an angry cat.

'The problem,' muttered Odd to himself, now determined not to be beaten, 'is how to open that door.'

From within the cupboard there was not a sound. Odd began to be alarmed in case whoever was inside had suffocated. What could he do?

He padded over to the flex and absent-mindedly pressed the switch on and off, as though sending out an SOS signal in morse code. If only he could loop the flex around the handle and then tug, he should be able to open the door.

He tried once, he tried twice. 'If at first you don't succeed, try, try again!' he muttered to himself, tugging away. One final jerk and the door of the cupboard opened. At the same moment the ceiling cracked, the light socket fell out, and Odd lay buried under a pile of plaster! He sat in the middle of the room, like a snowman, his nose unthreading.

'Atchoo! Atchoo!' came from the cupboard as the dust from the plaster filled the room. Odd turned to peer through the sudden fog and there, hanging upside down by one leg – the foot caught in a hook on the upper shelf – was a circus clown.

The clown had bright red wool hair, a red beaked nose and white face, beady black eyes, a yellow bow round the neck with a jewelled brooch in the centre, a red shirt covered with white spots, and candy-striped trousers!

'Atchoo!' sneezed the clown.

Odd, who still felt a little dazed by his fall, sat staring.

Suddenly the upside-down clown opened one eye and winked at him.

'You look like a chimpanzee!' observed Odd, then blushed brown because that sounded rather rude.

'So would you!' retorted the clown, 'if you were stuck up here and couldn't get down. Instead of making such footling and fatuous remarks, why don't you find a pole or something and push me off this hook!'

'But you'd break your neck!' exclaimed Odd.

'Not I!' answered the clown. 'For Falls, various and spectacular! All Jelly-Rolls, Back-Somersaults, Head-Stands, Hand-Stands, Cart-Wheels, you can't touch us! Even on the flying trapeze our family would never use the safety net. Why, we used to have all our bones broken before we were born!'

'That's all very well for you,' retorted Odd, 'but I'm bruised all over!'

He had decided the clown was rather conceited. Not one word of thanks had he received for getting the cupboard door open. Besides, now that he looked, the clown did not seem to be very uncomfortable. Indeed, he seemed to be enjoying his topsy-turvy state, and was singing to himself, swinging gently from side to side.

As the clown sang louder and louder, so he swung from side to side more and more vigorously. Suddenly his foot was loosened by the violent movement, and for the second time that day Odd found himself buried under an avalanche!

'Don't you think we ought to introduce ourselves?'

he said, extricating himself from the tangle of arms and legs. 'I'm Odd,' he added.

'You can say that again!' chuckled the clown. He sat up abruptly, throwing one floppy leg over the other, and leaned back on his hands, which were covered with white gloves. 'I'm Elsewhere!' he said loftily.

Outside in the street a barrel organ was playing, and in a moment Elsewhere had pulled Odd to his feet, and both were dancing round the room.

'Dedadedadedadeda!' sang Odd loudly.

'Lalalalalalala!' echoed Elsewhere, as they revolved faster and faster until, out of breath, they fell on the floor, laughing and giggling with delight.

'After all,' thought Odd, 'I'm not alone any more.'

TWO

'How did you come to get your name?' asked Odd. They were walking down the middle of the hedge that divided their garden from that of the house next door. Once upon a time there had been two hedges, but now they were so old and intertwined that down the centre there was a tunnel where blackbirds hopped among dead leaves, and wrens built their nest.

'It's a nickname really,' replied Elsewhere. 'My great-great-great (I forget how many greats) -great-grandfather was a clown and he went to Russia and became so famous that Queen Catherine the Great built him a private circus. He used to travel all over the world with that circus. One of his great-great-great (I forget how many greats) -great-grandsons was famous as a cannon ball king; he used to be shot out of a cannon, right over the circus ring. One day, he was sitting astride the cannon, smoking his cigar, when he accidentally dropped it down the muzzle and blew himself up!'

'Boom, boom, boom, bang!' went Odd. He jumped up into the air, then did a double somersault, rolling over and laughing. A blackbird was so startled that it flew up above the hedge with a loud chink-chink-chink-chink! It was such fun having a friend, thought Odd; someone with whom he could talk and exchange ideas.

'Of course, all circus people are really gipsies,' added Elsewhere. 'They are on the move the whole time, and they never stop in one place for very long. I'm always surprised to find myself where I am, and yet I am never surprised to find myself elsewhere. One moment you are top of the bill and famous; and the next you are stuffed in a cupboard and forgotten. You just get to feel, well – Elsewhere.'

Odd was very impressed by this, and tried to look serious and wise like Elsewhere; but he kept wanting to jump about and point out all sorts of exciting things to his new friend.

'I tell you what,' he said, swinging on a branch in the roof of the tunnel and getting his face caught in a spider's web, 'we'll go and find Collander Moll and ask her to give us some breakfast. And after that we'll go exploring.'

'Who's Collander Moll?' asked Elsewhere, picking up a feather left behind by the blackbird and sticking it in his hair.

'She's Hallelujah Jones's daughter. She does all the cooking and cleaning next door, while Hallelujah does all the gardening. He used to be a policeman in North Wales until he retired.'

At that moment they came to the end of the tunnel,

and Odd opened part of the hedge like a door. They stepped out into the next door garden. A bent old man was slowly raking up dead leaves and putting them on a large bonfire that was sending up clouds of smoke across all the other gardens.

'This is Hallelujah Jones!' announced Odd, stepping forward and introducing his friend.

Hallelujah straightened himself slowly and tilted his policeman's helmet on to the back of his head.

'How are you then, boy bach?' he said to Odd. Then looking at Elsewhere's brightly-coloured clothes and foreign appearance he crooked his fork in one arm, spat on a hand, wiped it on his jacket, and extended it to

Elsewhere. 'I thought you'd gone to Scotland then!
What happened?' he asked of Odd, reaching for his clay
pipe in the pocket in the tail of his coat.

'I got left behind. Elsewhere was shut in a cupboard
and I got him out. Now we're hungry! Can we come and
have some breakfast with you?'

'Look you now, come and have a bacon sandwich and
a cup of tea, boy bach! Moll's gone to the shops.' He lit
a twig from the bonfire and lighted his pipe which was
stuffed with dried coltsfoot. 'You can bring the wheelbarrow with you, if you'd like a job. Give you an
appetite for your breakfast!'

He chuckled and set off at a trot down the garden
path, his knobbly bow legs sticking out at right angles

to his bent body, and his long thin feet encased in leather wrappings. Odd leaped into the wheelbarrow, crying, 'Bags I a ride!' so Elsewhere had to push it. Bumpety-bump they went over the stones of the crazy paving, twisting in and out among forests of tall buttercups and waving green grass, and shrubberies full of thrushes, pecking and searching for worms and insects. Chink-chink-chink-chink! went the blackbird as it flew down the garden warning the other birds that they were coming.

They crossed a lawn under apple and plum trees, Elsewhere stopping to fill the barrow with windfalls until it was so heavy that Odd had to get out and help to push. They passed greenhouses, went along another lawn until they came to a tall house. This was Fenton House and it belonged to the National Trust which takes care of famous old houses. The house had a valuable collection of harpsichords, clavichords, spinets and virginals which students of the Royal College of Music were allowed to play. The house was always full of music and you could sit or stroll about and no one ever bothered you. Hallelujah led the way to the stone steps that went down to the basement where he and Collander Moll lived.

'I'll go and put the kettle on,' he said, 'while you bring in the plums. Just put them on the slate shelf in the pantry, and Moll will sort them out later.'

Collander Moll's kitchen was as warm as an oven and smelled of newly-baked bread. Hanging from the mantelpiece, in front of the fire, like lines of rags that have been washed and hung out to dry, were bunches of coltsfoot.

'When it's dry,' explained Odd, 'Hallelujah crumples it into a tin and uses it for tobacco.'

'It smells like a haystack,' sniffed Elsewhere as Hallelujah puffed away.

'Here, boy bach!' said Hallelujah, handing Odd a large round loaf. 'Cut some slices for yourself then while I fry the bacon.'

Elsewhere helped lay the table, and Hallelujah, his pipe still in his mouth, held a frying pan over the fire and prodded with a fork at the pieces of sizzling bacon.

'Doesn't he ever take off his helmet?' whispered Elsewhere.

The three sat round the kitchen table drinking mugs of strong tea, with lots of sugar for energy, and the two of them munching their bacon sandwiches.

'I had my breakfast earlier,' explained Hallelujah. He leaned forward to look at Odd and then got up and went over to the mantelpiece. He reached up and took down a bowl full of pencils, pieces of string, rubber bands, boxes of matches, all kinds of odds and ends, and finally a pair of steel-rimmed spectacles covered with dust from the fire. Wiping them on his sleeve he put them on and hobbled over to take another look at Odd.

'Hello, then! You been in the wars, boy bach? That nose of yours don't look too good to me. I'll get a needle and thread and we'll have you right in a jiffy.'

Until then Odd had forgotten about his nose, which had started to come unravelled when he had been helping Elsewhere get out of the cupboard.

Hallelujah shuffled back with a work basket and went to sit by the window, its sill crowded with pots of geraniums. A sleepy fly bumped and bounced against the window pane, caught between the glass and the net curtain.

'Come on over here then,' said Hallelujah, 'where I can see you.'

He took some cotton and, sucking the end, threaded it through a fine needle.

'This'll hurt, mind you,' he added, 'so you'd better count up to a hundred.'

Instead, Odd stared up into the acorn-coloured face of Hallelujah, trying to count how many wrinkles there were in his stained and worn velvety face with its bright beady eyes. His nose, stuck out at right angles like a thumb, had been stitched and re-stitched many times in different coloured threads. Hallelujah smelled of fire and tobacco smoke and unwashed clothes. He never went to bed but slept in the kitchen chair by the side of the fire.

Odd could feel the needle piercing his nose and the thread moving in and out, yet he felt no pain. He gazed up trustingly into the wise, old face of Hallelujah as he patiently sewed away, muttering to himself, 'Hallelujah! Praise the Lord! Amen! Hallelujah!'

Suddenly a door slammed. Odd jumped and yelped as

he jabbed hard against the needle; the kettle spat into the fire, and the robin outside flew away.

'Ah, that's Collander Moll!' laughed Hallelujah. 'She will charge around so. She never opens a door but she feels compelled to slam it. "I like to know I've come in, Dad," she says!'

At that moment the kitchen door blew open and Collander Moll burst in, laden with groceries, provisions, and a large coloured umbrella.

'Hullo, Dad!' she said. 'Having a party then? Who's this? What's our Odd been up to? Make us a cup of tea then, there's a dear!'

Questions and shopping spilled in all directions as she

bustled around, unwrapping parcels, emptying bags, passing in and out of the pantry. Elsewhere made a fresh pot of tea, while Hallelujah put the last stitches in Odd's nose, then bit off the end of the thread.

'You could do with a bit of a stitch yourself, Dad!' observed Collander Moll. 'That old arm of yours is coming loose again. Here, give me that needle!' and stopping in the middle of what she was doing, she proceeded to sew Hallelujah's left arm more securely to his body. 'There! that's better then,' she said.

'Well, take the needle out, girl,' grumbled Hallelujah. 'I don't want that stuck in my arm all day as though I were a pin-cushion. That's how you get pins and needles, as easy as that!'

Collander Moll removed her shiny black straw bonnet and stuck the pin into her hair which was piled up loosely like a jackdaw's nest, and held in place by an odd assortment of pins and needles and old hair-nets. Moll never bothered what she looked like, though she most resembled one of her own cottage loaves, a big lump of dough at the bottom with a small lump stuck on top. She would pull on any old clothes, a patchwork assortment of whatever was to hand, so that even if she were to fall downstairs, she would only go flumphety-flumph instead of flumpety-flump, and never get hurt!

She took a second look at Elsewhere's patchwork costume and laughed. 'There's a young man after my own heart. We could make a nice patchwork quilt between the two of us!'

23

Suddenly as they were laughing Elsewhere flopped into a faint on the floor. Collander Moll made up a bed for him in her room.

'After all,' she said in a motherly manner, 'if you'd been hanging upside down inside a cupboard for several days on end, you'd be exhausted too. He needs a long sleep, some good food, and to take things quietly. You've got to take care of him, Odd. No charging about, getting up to all kinds of mischief.'

Odd, feeling very abashed, tip-toed into the bedroom to look at his friend asleep in a small brass bedstead, in sheets smelling of lavender, his hair scarlet against the plumped-up pillows. Then he, too, exhausted by the morning's exertions, fell asleep in the chair at the side of the bed.

'Bless my soul!' whispered Collander Moll to her

father, on looking in to see what had happened to Odd. 'They're a pair of Babes in the Wood. They're both asleep. Well, Father, let's you and I leave them there.'

So back went Hallelujah to his garden, while Collander Moll, suddenly and attentively quiet, moved silently about her household chores, closing every door softly behind her, so that she should not waken Odd and Elsewhere. When she had done all her jobs, Collander Moll sat stitching away at a pair of trousers she was making for Odd out of one of the many aprons she wore tied around her waist. It was a faded blue denim that would stand up to the wear and tear of the many adventures of a small bear, from climbing trees to sliding down bannisters.

THREE

Odd awoke to the smell of carrots, onions, turnips, swedes and herbs, all simmering with beans and lentils in a pot on the stove. He knew without looking that there would be large, plump, shining dumplings bobbing about on the surface. The house was very quiet except for one student above practising on a spinet. He looked across at Elsewhere and saw that he was still asleep. He slipped quietly out of the room. There was no sign of Collander Moll although the table was laid for dinner. He opened the outer door and wandered into the garden in search of Hallelujah.

On the lawn a plump thrush was squatting in the bird-bath, turning round and round, ducking its head and beak into the water and tilting up its tail, then shaking its feathers as it came up for air, spilling-splashing the water in all directions. This done, it shifted to another point of the compass and repeated its performance all over again.

Odd found Hallelujah on the lower lawn, rubbing his hands with earth.

'What are you doing?' he inquired.

'Ah, there you are, boy bach!' he chuckled, as though Odd had just that moment popped up through the ground. 'You see those small mounds of earth all over the lawn? Them's mole hills. Them dratted moles will ruin that there lawn, so I'm going to set some traps for 'em. That'll soon stop their tricks.'

'But why are you rubbing your hands with soil?'

'That's so they won't smell my fingers as I set the traps. That's their own soil. So all they'll smell is mole.'

Odd followed Hallelujah around as he set the traps wherever the moles were still active.

27

'You mightn't realise it but under this lawn there's tunnels all over the place. Them moles can dig as much as thirty yards in one night with their little pink feet – like spades they are. If you imagine twenty moles in one night, that's two thousand feet! Underneath here –' he paused dramatically, taking his pipe from his mouth in order to emphasize what he was about to say – 'underneath here it's like Brixton Prison! There's a great central hall and round it are two galleries, one above the other, and from each of these there are tunnels going off in all directions. You have to fight these moles like a disease. They're worse than couch grass, and that's bad enough. Otherwise you could come out here one morning and walk across the lawn and suddenly it could all cave in under you. It's like everything else,' he added philosophically, 'you have to tread softly. You never know when the ground is going to give way beneath you. Life's full of danger, boy. You can't stand under a tree to shelter from a storm but you may get struck by lightning – it goes zig-zag across the sky, suddenly it sees the tree, down it goes, and tree and you have had it. I reckon as all tall trees ought to have lightning conductors fixed to 'em, like up on our chimney there. Anyway, at least there's one good thing we don't have in England, or bad thing more like, and that's volcanoes.'

'What's that?'

'A volcano is a great mountain that's had its inside scooped out. It's full of lava, a hot liquid, all simmering away – like one of Moll's stews on the stove. That's what a volcano is – a big stew on the stove. And every hundred years or so it boils over and causes a lot of trouble. Mind you, you can get knocked down crossing the road – even if you do look both ways. You can slip on the ice and break your ankle. You can be sitting at home and all of a sudden the ceiling falls in on you. Ah, it's best not to stir a foot, although even then you'd get pins and needles. Life's full of perils, boy bach.'

Odd stood there, filled with gloom at the thought. Suddenly Hallelujah winked at him and they both laughed.

'You mustn't believe everything I say,' chuckled Hallelujah.

They carried the unused traps back to the greenhouse. At one end were kept all the tools – a brass watering-can with a long spout, a besom – a broom made of twigs tied to a pole for sweeping up leaves – rakes and spades, forks and hoes, dibbers and shears and garden-mowers. On a line above the stove hung more coltsfoot leaves. On the wall to one side of the stove Odd noticed a lot of small, black furry skins stretched and drying.

'Them's moles!' grinned Hallelujah. 'As I catch 'em I skin 'em! Come Christmas there'll be enough for a fur coat for Moll, but don't ee tell 'er, it's to be a surprise.'

Odd sat on an upturned bucket and leaned against a string of onions.

'Collander Moll, Collander Moll!' he chanted to himself. He really wanted to ask Hallelujah how she came

to have a name like that but didn't like to ask. He looked up at the old policeman who was now examining trays of seeds that were beginning to sprout in their shallow beds of soil. Hallelujah grinned at him.

'You know what is a Colander?' he said, his voice rising at the end of the sentence with a Welsh lilt. 'It's what you put the vegetables in when you drain away

the water – it's an enamel bowl full of holes. Well now, our Moll was always so scatter-brained, never could remember anything, that our Mam used to say – "Her brain's like a colander, full of holes!" She'd plant seeds and forget where she'd planted them. She'd go to post a letter and put the front-door key in the pillar-box by mistake. She'd go to church in her night-dress and her curlers still in her hair. She'd put on a kettle or a sauce-pan full of water and you'd come back to find 'em boiled dry. She used to say, "the only way to make custard is to let it boil over." She was like a squirrel, always for-getting where she'd put things. She'd find money under the carpet or in a jam-jar and forget she'd ever put it there. Our Mam used to send her out on an errand and she'd forget what she'd been sent for. "There's always so much to see, Dad," she'd say. "I'll never have time to see it all." We used to tease her and say she'd forget to turn up for her own wedding – and that's why she never married.'

'Do you think she's forgotten it's dinner time?' asked Odd.

Hallelujah paused, looked at him, reached his earth-stained fingers into his uniform pocket and took out a turnip watch.

'Right you are, boy bach!' he nodded. 'She's forgotten all right!'

And with that they hurried along the gravel path, up the steps to the upper lawn, down the steps to the base-ment, and into the kitchen where they found Elsewhere sitting at the table, a large napkin tied around his neck, banging at the table with his knife and fork and saying, 'I'm hungry!'

FOUR

For dinner Odd and Elsewhere had vegetable stew, followed by apple pie, full of cloves, and with lots of ice-cream melting all over the top. After dinner Odd tried on his new trousers, and jumped up and down with delight. He thrust his hands into the pockets and pulled out from one pocket a bright, tangerine-coloured handkerchief, and from the other a shining silver five pence

piece. Collander Moll laughed and said, 'Now, Odd, you must take care of Elsewhere, and don't get into any trouble!'

To Elsewhere she whispered, 'Keep an eye on Odd and see he doesn't get up to any mischief!'

She gave them her large coloured umbrella – 'in case it rains' – and waved them off. They ran up the basement steps, crossed the lawn, went down a gravel path and through the tall iron gates that led out into the street.

The wind blew bits of paper scudding and leaping and tumbling along the road. Some large drops of rain splashed on to Elsewhere's nose.. He opened the umbrella and holding it in front of them the two friends walked downhill. Suddenly the wind grabbed hold of

the umbrella and the next minute they found them-
selves floating over the garden of Fenton House. Collander Moll, looking through the window to see if her
father was sheltering from the rain, saw the two
parachuting across the garden. Seizing a coat she ran
out of the house, shouting up at them. At the same time
Hallelujah emerged from the greenhouse, an old sack
draped over his head to protect him from the rain. Odd
and Elsewhere did not dare to wave as the umbrella
zig-zagged on its course, switchbacking up and down in
the drenching rain. Now they were sailing over Hampstead Heath, and on the skyline they could see St Paul's
Cathedral, and beyond that the hills of Surrey. The rain
stopped and the clouds cleared. The sun shone and dried
out their wet clothes, but still the wind blew them along.

35

'Oh, dear! Oh, dear!' cried Odd.

'What is it?' asked Elsewhere, who at that moment had been practising loop-the-loop.

'I'm afraid I'm going to fall, like I did this morning. You see, I don't have a very strong grip,' sobbed Odd.

Elsewhere wrapped both his long legs around Odd, so that even if he did let go of the umbrella Odd would still be safe.

'Do you see that place underneath us?' said Odd. 'That's an animal prison. If I were to fall in there I'd be locked up in a cage, and I'd never be let out and people would come and stare at me. It's called a shoe.'

'You mean a Zoo,' commented Elsewhere.

'Do I?' replied Odd.

Peering down between his arms and over Odd's head, Elsewhere could see stretches of water, a great cage with no birds in it, penguins swimming in a blue pool, elephants, bears, giraffes, kangaroos, zebras, and people wandering about with ice-creams and cameras. At times it was difficult to tell whether the people were looking at the animals or the animals looking at the people.

As soon as they were past the Zoo and over Regent's Park, Odd began to feel more cheerful. The wind had slackened and they were flying closer to the ground. People passing below pointed them out and said, 'Oh, look – it's an advertisement for something!' They slid down the wind towards a sloping lawn with rows and rows of deck-chairs, surrounded by high trees and hedges. The seats were full of school children and they

were all watching a group of men on a grassy mound who were wearing old-fashioned clothes and speaking a funny kind of language in a very loud voice as though everyone were deaf.

'What is it?' whispered Odd. 'Is it a church service?'

'No,' answered Elsewhere, who knew all about this sort of thing. 'It's an open-air theatre and they're performing a play by William Shakespeare.'

'But why are they shouting?'

'That's so the people at the back can hear them. Only it isn't shouting really. It's what's called – *projecting*. It's the same in the circus ring. You have to learn how to project your voice so that the people in the back can hear.'

Because they were so busy talking they had forgotten to look where they were going. Suddenly they bumped into the top of a tall plane tree. The sudden jolt made Elsewhere loosen his legs and Odd, who had let go of the handle of the umbrella, went tumbling down, head over heels, round and round.

'O monstrous! O strange!' declaimed a voice below. 'We are haunted. Pray, masters! Fly, masters! Help!'

It was at this point that Odd landed with a bump on the stage. The actors stopped speaking all of a sudden. The children in the audience began to laugh and to jump up and down with excitement in their damp seats.

'What is it?' asked one of the actors.

'It's a teddy-bear! I suppose it belongs to one of the kids in the audience.'

'Well, chuck it back,' hissed the large actor who was

playing the part of Bottom in *A Midsummer Night's Dream*. 'Let's get on with the play.'

'They like a bit of slap-stick,' rejoined the other actor who was playing Puck. He took hold of Odd by one arm and sent him hurling out over the audience. All the children, hundreds of them, stood up, trying to catch Odd.

'Let's have a look! Let's have a look!' they shouted, as Odd was thrown from one part of the audience to another. He was beginning to feel very dizzy and sick when suddenly Elsewhere, who had been watching from the top of the tree, created a diversion. He began to somersault downwards from branch to branch, performing double turns in mid-air, like a man on a flying trapeze.

'Oh, look! Look!' shouted all the children, their eyes caught by the bright flash of his hair and costume. They began to cheer and for a moment, in their new excitement, Odd was forgotten.

The play had come to a standstill and the actors stood around, not knowing what to do. An important-looking man came down the aisle, shouting angrily, 'Get down from there at once, you young hooligan!'

Under cover of the commotion Odd had slipped away, hidden behind the tree, waiting for Elsewhere who now slid down to the bottom, panting and out of breath. Grabbing Odd's paw he said, 'Come on! Let's scarper!'

And the two friends ran without stopping past flower-beds and elderly people on benches in the sunlight; over a bridge with water underneath; past Madame Tussaud's and all her wax-works, until they came to Baker Street where Sherlock Holmes, the famous detective, used to live. Here they flopped down on a pavement and watched the traffic go by, until they had got back their breath.

FIVE

'Where are all those people going?' asked Elsewhere, scratching at his leg.

'That's the Tube,' answered Odd. Then seeing Elsewhere's puzzled look he explained further. 'The Tube is a tunnel that goes underground all over London. It's like the moles under Hallelujah's lawn. There's tunnels all over the place. You go down a tunnel and get on a train which takes you to wherever you want to go. There are different trains for different places, and sometimes you have to change from one train to another. Then you come up to the surface, just like a rabbit coming up out of its burrow.'

'Do you have to pay?' asked Elsewhere, now scratching at the other leg.

'Well, yes,' replied Odd. 'Otherwise you might get arrested. They have people in wooden sentry-boxes who check your tickets when you go in and as you come out at the other end.'

Elsewhere was looking rather thoughtful. 'But if we were to pretend to be with someone,' he said, 'would we have to pay then?'

'No, I don't think so. You mean if we were to tag on to someone then we could slip past, almost without being noticed?'

'For instance,' replied Elsewhere, springing to his feet, 'if we were to follow that little girl with the pigtails and the satchel everybody would think we were with her!'

'You don't think she's too old for a teddy-bear?' asked Odd, somewhat dubiously.

But Elsewhere did not wait to reply, and grabbing Odd by the paw he was hurrying along behind the small girl, until they had passed the ticket barrier, and were running across a metal bridge and down some steps on to a crowded platform.

'That was easy,' laughed Odd. 'Oh, look! Here's a train! Come on!'

'But where is it going?' asked Elsewhere, who was

42

much more practical than Odd, and for whom the only point in getting on a train was in order to travel somewhere. Odd, however, would have been perfectly happy to have gone anywhere just for the ride.

'It goes round and round in a circle,' he explained. 'That's why it's called the Inner Circle. You can stay on it all day if you want to, and even if you paid you wouldn't have to spend any more.'

Each time the train stopped they got out and moved into the next compartment, in order to look at the advertisements and see what different people there were. By the time they had reached Westminster Station they were in the front compartment behind the engine driver. At Victoria they decided to get off and wait for the next Circle train.

'Shall we have some chocolate?' said Odd, untying the handkerchief in which he had put his five pence piece for safety. 'I'm very hungry.'

So Elsewhere climbed up on to Odd's back in order to reach the chocolate machine, and put in his new coin for a bar of chocolate. They heard the money fall down inside the machine, and Elsewhere tugged at the drawer which was supposed to contain the chocolate. The drawer was stuck! He pressed the button marked 'Money back' but nothing happened. He banged on the machine. He climbed down off Odd's shoulders.

'Something's stuck!' he said.

Just at that moment the train came in.

'Hurry up!' shouted Odd, running towards it.

The doors started to close and a boy inside grabbed hold of his arm to pull him on board.

'Stop!' shouted Elsewhere, grabbing Odd's other arm. At that moment the arm pulled by the boy came off; Odd and Elsewhere fell back on the platform; the doors closed and the train moved off, with Odd's arm *inside*.

He looked at the black thread trickling down where his arm ought to be, and burst into tears.

'It's your fault!' he sobbed, hitting Elsewhere violently on the nose and hoping it would bleed. But it only squashed and then popped back into place again. Odd was now in a dreadful temper.

44

'That's the trouble with clowns,' he shouted. 'They're so boneless and spineless! Now we've got no money and no chocolate and I've got no arm!'

'If you hadn't been in such a hurry,' said Elsewhere calmly (which only infuriated Odd the more), 'we might not have been in this predicament.'

' 'Ere, 'ere! What's all this about?' asked a kindly, squeaky voice. They looked up and saw an elderly, walrus-moustached guard, lifting his hat in astonishment and scratching the back of his balding head. 'We can't 'ave two young beatniks like you disturbing the peace! What's up, like?'

So they explained, and the guard tugged at his moustache and scratched at his shiny scalp.

'Do you think,' sniffed Odd, 'that if we were just to wait here, the train might come round again with my arm in it?'

'Maybe happen it would,' replied the guard – and at once Odd began to cheer up. 'Then, again, maybe happen it wouldn't. You see, for all us know, someone might take a fancy to that there arm, and take it 'ome with them, for a kind of souvenir, like. Arter all,' he sniffed again, ' 'tain't every day one finds a bear's arm. Nope! Howsomever, I reckon as you'd better come along with us, and us'll see what us can do, like.'

He led them through a door in the wall, and along a passage; through another door, and another door, and yet another door; then down some steps, and into a glass-walled control room, full of levers and switches

45

and time-tables and clocks. Elsewhere climbed up on to a chair and looked out through the windows.

'What are all those women doing?' he asked.

Odd stood on tip-toe and managed to peer over the sill. They looked out on to a large arena into which all the tunnels converged. The arena was like the hub of a wheel and the tunnels like the spokes.

Down the various tunnels came hundreds of women in old clothes, with scarves tied round their heads, and some with hats perched on top. They were carrying bags and bundles and brooms and buckets and dusters and mops, which they set down as soon as they arrived at the space in the centre. Some took out methylated spirit stoves which they pumped up, lit, and then boiled

kettles of water on to make pots and flasks of tea. Others took out bottles of stout and bread-and-cheese-and-pickle sandwiches. One chewed a cucumber. Some put down newspapers and went to sleep. Others opened newspapers and read them. Some folded their newspapers and did the crossword puzzle. Some knitted. Some played cards. One even smoked a pipe.

'Ah! Them's the cleaners!' explained the old guard. 'You'm lucky to see them. Not many do. They'll settle down here till the trains stop running. Then, when everyone else is in bed, fast asleep, they all go off in platoons to their different tunnels, and push those long brooms you can see. They sweep up all the rubbish people throw down on the lines. Others wash and scrub

and polish and dust until it is all bright and sparkling
for the first train in the morning. Then they go off to
their homes and start washing, scrubbing, dusting and
polishing, all over again. Them's the cleaners. I don't
know what us 'ld do without 'em. Now then,' he con-
cluded. 'Let's see what us can do about this 'ere arm of
yours, like. While I make some telephone calls, why
don't you help yourselves to some tea off the stove,
like.'

Odd and Elsewhere, sipping tea, stood on the table
and watched the cleaners arriving. There must have
been eight or nine hundred of them. It was like watching
an army assemble.

'They all look a bit like Collander Moll,' whispered
Elsewhere, and Odd giggled.

After a lot of telephoning, the old guard with the
yellow-stained whiskers, announced, 'Well, laddie!
You're in luck. It seems your arm were 'anded in at the
Lost Property Office in Oxford Street about 'alf an
hour ago.' He wheezed and began to chuckle. 'Looks
like it ain't come to no 'arm, 'asn't your arm! Ha, ha,
ha!'

Elsewhere tickled Odd under his one arm to make
him laugh and in a minute all three were laughing at
the guard's joke. Then an empty train pulled in at one
of the sidings; the guard put them on board, instructing
the driver to take them to Oxford Circus.

Odd and Elsewhere thanked their friend, and got on
the train. To their excitement it drove through all the

stations without stopping. They ran up and down the train, looking out at all the people crowded on the platforms, wondering why an empty train should be hurtling along, bearing only a shabby-looking clown and a one-armed teddy-bear.

SIX

At Oxford Street a railway official, with gold braid on
his cap, met them and showed them the way to the
Lost Property Office. Up and down the street outside
shuffled old men carrying sandwich-boards advertising
the Lost Property Office.

They pushed open a glass door and entered a large room like a library, divided by tall shelves reaching to the ceiling. The shelves were crowded with all the things people lose on trains. They were all marked alphabetically, and there were sections for: False Teeth, Male and Female; Spectacles, Ancient and Modern; Shoes, High-Heeled, Flat, Gear. At one end they saw a line of doors marked: Mothers, Infants, Fathers, Nurse-Maids, Helpless Aunts, Anxious Uncles. Then there were a series of dog kennels marked: Thorough-Bred Dogs, Mongrel Dogs, Toy Dogs, Shaggy Dogs, Lame Dogs. Standing in the fireplace, its neck going up the chimney (as it was too tall to stand in the room), was

a solitary Giraffe. Hanging from the ceiling were hundreds and hundreds of umbrellas.

Elsewhere led the way to the shelves marked 'A'.

'But how shall we go about finding it?' asked Odd. 'I mean "A" stands for Apple, Antimacassar, Antelope, Antler, Apron, Astrachan, Aubretia, and – oh, lots of other things. We might be all day looking for my Arm.'

Suddenly he sighed and flopped down on the floor, quite exhausted. He had never before realized just how much lost property there was in the world. And how was he to find one small arm amongst all that?

'Besides,' he added to Elsewhere with sudden alarm, 'it might be under "B" for Bear, or "T" for Teddy-Bear!'

At that moment they heard a voice high above them wheeze and say, 'W-hot can I do for you, gentlemen?' pronouncing the 'h' as though the speaker had a hot potato in his mouth. Looking up they saw, mounted on top of a tall library ladder, a very fat gentleman with three chins, bristly hair and large black bushy eyebrows.

'We've come about my friend's lost arm,' announced Elsewhere.

The ladder creaked and swayed, and Odd ran round the corner in fright. Slowly, like a black cloud descending, the fat man wheezed his way down, with a smell of moth-balls and snuff.

'On w-hot train did you lose w-hot arm?' he asked, looming up at a high desk in a corner of the room. He opened a large, leather-bound ledger. He pushed his horn-rimmed spectacles up on to his forehead and, placing his white hands one on top of the other in front of him, peered down at them over the desk.

'It was on the Inner Circle,' explained Elsewhere, taking charge. 'It came off at Victoria, about an hour ago, and we were told to report here.'

The fat man peered down closer at Odd (who was trying to hide behind Elsewhere), and grew a fourth chin.

'The Arm of the Law!' he announced in a magisterial voice.

'No, sir! Please, sir! *My* arm!' stuttered Odd.

'The Arm of the Law!' intoned the fat man, straightening up and losing three chins. 'It was handed in by the arm of the law! Police Constable Higgins of the Walthamstow Constabulary was on his way back home when he discovered the aforementioned arm and handed it in. Now, let me see, under w-hot did we file it? It's not often,' he added, 'that we get an arm. An artificial leg, yes. You'd be surprised how careless people are. They take out their false teeth, unstrap their limbs, remove their wigs – oh, you've no idea!'

He paused and then, with surprising agility, stooped down and took hold of Odd's arm.

'Careful!' yelped Odd, alarmed lest he should now lose the other arm. He was feeling distinctly groggy after such a long day. All the exertions of the morning, rescuing Elsewhere; their being parachuted across London and his nearly falling into the Zoo; his being thrown about at the open-air theatre – which was when his arm must have worked loose – *and* his cold! he suddenly remembered; he'd forgotten about that.

'Atchoo! Atchoo!' he sneezed, as though to remind himself.

'He's feeling rather sensitive, I think,' explained Elsewhere to the fat man. 'He doesn't mean to be rude.'

The fat man took from the desk a telescope and pulling it out to its fullest extent examined Odd's arm.

'Arbuthnot!' he declaimed loudly. 'Lot number 2316207468999.'

There was a silence and then they heard a click and

a trapdoor in the floor pushed up. Through it, climbing up from below, came a dwarf carrying a cardboard shoe-box, with a label tied to it marked 'Lot 2316207468999'. Arbuthnot handed the box to the fat man, winked at Odd and Elsewhere, then climbed back down his ladder, until he was standing with his head on a level with the floor, and the trap-door resting on the top of his head.

'W-hot have we here?' soliloquized the fat man, opening the cardboard box.

'Oh, please, sir! Yes, sir! That's my arm!' cried Odd excitedly.

'Ah, but have you any identification? Eh? How am I to know, how are *we* to know if, in fact, this is *your* arm? Some other bear might have lost his arm in the Great Metropolis, and it wouldn't do to get them all mixed up now, would it? You wouldn't like to have some other bear's arm, would you?'

'But Mr Like told us you had it here,' replied Elsewhere.

'Like?' boomed the fat man.

'Do you mean, "Us'll 'ave to see what us can do, like"?' queried Arbuthnot.

'Yes, that's right,' laughed Odd.

'Well, why didn't you say so in the first place. That will be five pence, please.'

And so saying, the fat man began to wrap up Odd's arm in brown paper. He handed the parcel, with a low bow, and an extra chin, to Elsewhere.

'Oh, p-p-please!' stammered Odd. 'We haven't got any money! We – put – all – we – had – in – a – chocolate – machine – on – the – platform – and – it – went and – got – stuck – and – we – didn't – get – any – chocolate – or – our – money – back!'

'What do you think, Arbuthnot?' questioned the fat man, looking down at the dwarf, whose chin was resting on the floor at their feet.

'Might I suggest, sir,' said Arbuthnot solemnly, 'that, in this instance, the British Railways may be said to have been paid for services rendered? – albeit in an unorthodox manner. After all,' he added with a grin, 'we do do rather well out of those machines – if you come to think of all the lost five pence pieces we collect from them!'

'An excellent point, Arbuthnot. Your logic is as impeccable as ever,' observed the fat man. 'If you would just sign this receipt,' he added, handing a slip of paper to Elsewhere and waiting while he signed his name. Extending his hand, he then shook Odd gently by his one arm. 'Do call in any time you have both arms free. Arbuthnot and I will be only too delighted to see you and your friend from elsewhere.'

'No, no!' explained Odd. 'My friend's name is Elsewhere.'

'Much the same thing!' declared the fat man loftily.

The trap-door rose and Arbuthnot stepped out. Psst! Psst! he went, like a sudden escape of gas. He climbed up a ladder until he was on a level with the fat man's ear and whispered something to him. The fat man began to wobble and laugh.

'Stop it, Arbuthnot!' he cried. 'You're tickling me! Try again, only not so close.'

'Ps-ps-ps-ps-ps-ps-ps!' went Arbuthnot.

'Yes, yes, yes, yes, yes, yes, yes!' nodded the fat man in agreement and both their heads swung round to look at the two friends.

'Once again Arbuthnot hits the nail on the head. He points out to me that really you ought to get that arm seen to, else you may lose it again. He reminds me that the Royal Dolls' Hospital exists especially for such emergencies as this. He will escort you there. I, alas! am too large ever to leave this building. When first I entered that door I was a much slimmer and younger man; but now Arbuthnot has to take care of all my

needs. You will find him most helpful. My compliments to you, and good night! Perhaps, Arbuthnot, you would be so kind as to put up the "Closed" sign on your way out? I don't expect that we shall have any more callers today. I shall sit in the window and watch you go down the street.'

As they left, they could see the fat man winding up an old gramophone with a large, red horn. They could hear the cracked voice of a record playing the song 'All Alone By The Telephone'. And then the door closed.

SEVEN

'If you wouldn't mind waiting a few minutes,' said
Arbuthnot, 'I have to pay the sandwich-board men
their money. It's Friday and that means pay-day.'

In a yard at the back, overlooked by blocks of offices
were six men, taking off their sandwich-boards and
stacking them in a shed. When they had all signed for
their wages, Odd and Elsewhere were surprised to see
them break into a dance.

> In and out,
> arm in arm,
> up and down,
> forwards
> and
> backwards,

the sandwich-board men danced,

> stamping the ground with their feet,
>   clapping their hands,
> flourishing their handkerchiefs,
> and ringing the bells they had put on their
>   legs.

While they danced, one, with his pay-packet stuck in
the band of an old top-hat on the back of his head,
tapped out the rhythm with his foot and squeezed out
a vigorous tune on an accordion.

At the windows of the offices round about, all the
workers, preparing to go home, gathered to watch the
dancing. Windows opened out or slid up and people
threw money down into the yard.

'It's raining pennies!' laughed Odd, jumping up and
down in rhythm to the music since he was unable to
clap his paws.

The dancing stopped and everyone at the windows,

up, up, as high as you could look, and all around, applauded. The accordionist took off his top hat and collected the pennies which littered the yard, while the others mopped their faces with bright-coloured handkerchiefs.

'Right then! Let's go and have a drink!' said the men.

'Always on Fridays that happens,' explained Arbuthnot. 'As regular as clockwork. It's called Morris dancing. Now, if you wait a minute while I get out my machine, I'll give you a ride.'

They watched while Arbuthnot put on a fireman's brass helmet and a pair of goggles. Then he pulled out of the shed an old-fashioned tricycle, with a soap box on pram wheels at the back.

'Hop in!' he said, and with a sudden perilous lurch

the tricycle moved out of the yard, down a narrow passage, and into Oxford Street. At Oxford Circus the policeman on duty saluted Arbuthnot and, stopping all the traffic, waved them on into Regent Street.

'It's like being in the circus again,' remarked Elsewhere. 'Always, between the big acts – the elephants, performing dogs, dancing ponies, trapeze artists and jugglers – the clowns come on in funny costumes, riding bicycles and throwing water over each other, to make people laugh.'

'I hope nobody's going to throw water over us,' replied Odd apprehensively, looking up at the sky.

At Piccadilly Circus they turned into Leicester Square, and were just going down St Martin's Lane when Odd shouted out, 'Oh, look!'

Arbuthnot put on the brakes abruptly, and Odd and Elsewhere in the soap box were jerked forward. Arbuthnot climbed down, removing his goggles, and taking off his leather gloves.

'What is it?' he inquired with concern, thinking that perhaps Odd's other arm had fallen off.

'Oh, please, I'm awfully sorry! It isn't anything important. Only look there!'

They had stopped outside the New Theatre in St Martin's Lane. A queue of people were sitting on wooden stools under a hanging sign marked 'Gallery'. The queue stretched round the corner and up a side passage. The people in the queue were waiting to get into the gallery, right up under the roof of the theatre, which was where the cheap seats were. But what had caught Odd's eye was a shabby-looking man who was doing a soft-shoe shuffle dance in the side passage. In each hand he had a spoon and with these he was tapping out a tune on strips of metal tied to his stomach. It was as though he had taken a xylophone apart and hung the pieces round his waist.

'Oh, let's go and watch!' pleaded Odd.

So Arbuthnot tied a padlock to his tricycle so that it shouldn't be stolen, and they crossed the street to watch. Elsewhere helped Odd up on to a dustbin, so that he could see more easily. Arbuthnot went off to buy an evening paper.

Both Elsewhere and Odd observed how when the little man had finished his dance, he folded up an old newspaper into a purse, and then went along the queue collecting money.

'It's like the sandwich-board men,' said Odd excitedly.

'It's called busking,' explained Elsewhere. 'A busker is a man who entertains people in the street, outside a theatre or a cinema.'

Now another busker appeared who, without speaking, made mysterious signs to the gallery queue. He held up an enamel tin plate and showed it to the audience. Next, he took from his pocket a penny candle and displayed that. Finally he produced a box of matches, lit the candle, and everyone applauded. Now he held the tin plate over the candle flame until it was all black from the smoke. He blew out the candle and put it back in his pocket. With the end of the matchstick he began to draw a picture on the plate. The gallery queue, except for one man who sat on his stool reading a book, watched, fascinated. Even Arbuthnot, who had been reading the football results, lowered his newspaper. Slowly, in white lines on black, there appeared on the plate the picture of a steamship sailing across waves. Everyone clapped and applauded. The busker took round the plate, and those who hadn't given anything to the xylophone man gave something to him.

Odd looked round and saw Elsewhere whispering earnestly to Arbuthnot and tugging at his newspaper.

'But I haven't read it yet! Oh, really! I don't think you ought,' he exclaimed. 'After all, you haven't got a licence and you might be arrested.'

Elsewhere was busy folding the newspaper into a purse as he had observed the first busker do, and now he was whispering something to Odd. He handed the brown paper parcel, containing Odd's arm, to Arbuthnot.

Odd banged his feet and piped as loud as he could, 'Ladies and gentlemen!' He paused, and everyone turned to look in astonishment at a small, rather shabby, one-armed teddy-bear addressing them. 'I now have great privilege in presenting to you the most unique act ever to be seen in London! By that – that – that – '

He hesitated and Elsewhere hissed, 'Renowned – '

' – by that renowned and world-famous clown, Elsewhere! For all jelly-rolls,' he continued, 'back somersaults, head-stands, hand-stands, cart-wheels, he cannot be surpassed in London, England, Europe, the World, the Universe! Even on the trapeze he refuses to use a hair-net – '

'A safety net, you idiot!' muttered Elsewhere.

'He has not a bone in his body,' continued Odd undaunted. 'He is the world's most boneless clown!'

With a leap and a spring Elsewhere cart-wheeled down the side passage, then performed a series of back somersaults. Next he seized the lid off the dust-bin – so that Odd, who was taken by surprise, nearly fell into it – and up-ending it like a wheel, stood balanced on the rim and with quick, shuffling movements of the feet, began to perform figures-of-eight, drawing shouts of 'bravo!' from the audience. While he did this Odd was busy taking round the newspaper purse. It soon became so full of pennies and other copper and silver pieces, that his arm began to ache with the weight, and so he called to Arbuthnot to come and help. Arbuthnot, somewhat reluctantly, removed his fireman's helmet and used that to collect the money, while Odd went and picked up the brown paper parcel with his arm in it, in case someone should think it was rubbish and throw it away in the dustbin.

Just then all the people began to move into the theatre. Elsewhere, Odd and Arbuthnot sat on the pavement – and emptied the contents of Arbuthnot's helmet. They counted their takings, which came to sixty-three pence, an old threepeny bit, one Irish halfpenny and a brass button!

'That will come in rather handy,' commented Arbuthnot, putting the brass button to one side as his share of the takings. The rest they placed in the centre of Odd's orange-coloured handkerchief, knotted the ends together, and placed for safety inside Odd's trouser pocket.

It was now quite dark and all the lamps in the streets were lit.

'We're almost there,' said Arbuthnot cheerfully, as

the two friends climbed aboard. 'The Royal Dolls'
Hospital is only round the corner, at Charing Cross.
So we haven't far to go.' Stretching out his right arm
to signal to the traffic behind, he pedalled off down
St Martin's Lane and into Trafalgar Square where the
pigeons flew round Nelson's Column, and people with
cameras climbed over the lions at the foot.

As they rolled along, Elsewhere laughed and said,
'It's like being in a royal carriage. Look at all those
people waving at us.' And he and Odd waved back at
them.

'Do you think if we rode up to Buckingham Palace
we could have supper with the Queen?' asked Odd.

But instead of going up the Mall, Arbuthnot wheeled
sharply past St Martin-in-the-Fields, and trundled along
the Strand until they came to Amroyds Street and there,
ahead of them, in large gilt letters all across the front
of a building, they saw the words: THE ROYAL DOLLS'
HOSPITAL.

EIGHT

'It's like a dolls' house!' exclaimed Odd.

'That's exactly what it is,' replied Arbuthnot. 'It was built originally for the Queen and her sister when they were young, and now it has been turned into a dolls' hospital. Dolls from all over the world come here, it is so famous. It is open day and night.'

They went up the steps and in at the main entrance. Arbuthnot spoke quietly to the smart-looking receptionist, and in no time at all they were being taken up in a lift to a large drawing-room where they were asked to wait for Dr Solomon Tump. In the centre of the room was a round pedestal table, covered with magazines and periodicals. All round the room were leather arm-chairs, and by the window a deep comfortable sofa. It was a high room with a chandelier hanging from the ceiling in the centre.

Odd sat upright, perched on the edge of the sofa, feeling very awed, and clutching at his arm in its brown paper parcel. Arbuthnot, who had removed his helmet and goggles downstairs, took out a pair of spectacles and sat looking at a copy of *Punch*. Elsewhere flicked

through all the magazines very quickly, not stopping to read them, just looking at the pictures.

Arbuthnot peered over the top of his spectacles and looked at the magazines now thrown in disorder all over the table. He coughed quietly. 'I do think that, er, perhaps you might leave the reading matter as you found it, don't you know.'

'Oh, what a bore!' replied Elsewhere sulkily.

He had enjoyed being suddenly the centre of attention, with everyone applauding and shouting bravo! It had been quite like the old days in the circus ring. Before he had been thrown on a shelf in a cupboard and forgotten. He sat now on an upright chair and tapped the floor impatiently with his foot. 'How much longer is this doctor going to be?' he yawned rather loudly.

At that moment, to Arbuthnot's relief, a young woman entered and said with a smile, 'Would Mr Odd mind stepping this way, please.'

Elsewhere, who had also got up, expecting to go along with him, was somewhat disconcerted by this. He was quite surprised to see Odd march off on his own, trailing his brown paper parcel behind him, without even saying, 'Please, can I bring my friend, Elsewhere?' He flopped back on his chair and lolled there, looking *very* bored and dissatisfied.

'After all,' he grumbled, 'we didn't have to come here. Hallelujah or Collander Moll could just as easily have stitched on his arm again.'

'Who are they?' asked Arbuthnot politely.

'Oh, just some people we happen to be staying with,' replied Elsewhere loftily, still lying slumped in his chair. 'You may have heard of the place,' he continued. 'Fenton House. In Hampstead. I believe it's quite well known. It's one of those National Trust Places.' He flopped one leg over the other and tossed back his long shredded hair.

'Oh, indeed yes!' said Arbuthnot. 'It is a place frequently employed for musical soirées. Do you play?' he added almost without a pause, thereby disconcerting Elsewhere.

'I have strummed in my time,' he replied, abruptly

71

standing on his head. 'But not what you would call –
play. Play the fool, of course,' he added with a grin,
suddenly doing a hand-stand, then vaulting over and
on to the floor with a flourish.

'I wonder?' he said to himself, looking up at the
chandelier.

'Oh, I – I – er, I don't think – '

Arbuthnot failed to say what he did not think,
because at that moment Elsewhere cart-wheeled across
the room, sprang on to the table and, leaping up,
grabbed hold of one of the glass pendants of the
chandelier. The room tinkled and rang with the cas-

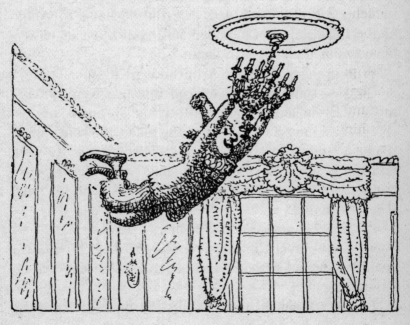

cading notes of all the pieces of glass shivering and colliding with each other.

Around the room were oval-shaped gilt mirrors, surmounted by cherubs, and as Elsewhere swung backwards and forwards, so he was reflected many times in the mirrors. And not only reflected once but doubly, trebly, quadruply, and many more times; each mirror reflecting the reflection of the mirror opposite, and the reflection within that, and the reflection within the reflection of the reflection reflecting the opposite reflection of the reflection within the reflection, and so on, until the room seemed full of swinging clowns.

Elsewhere was now performing the loop-the-loop, which was his speciality, and as he swayed and swung, so he lifted his legs and kicked at the glass pendants. The sound was like a thousand glass harmonicas amplified, played by mischievous musicians. Arbuthnot was so agitated that he ran backwards and forwards and around, getting dizzier and dizzier.

Ching-a-ling! ching-ching! and ching-a-chink-chink! went the pendants. Suddenly Arbuthnot dived under the table and crouched, holding on to the leg of the table. In the mirrors he could see the ceiling crack and the chain supporting the chandelier begin to slide. There was a splash of colour all round the room, reflected in all the mirrors – the colours of Elsewhere's patchwork clothes, and the many colours reflected in the pendants of the chandelier. The next moment the chandelier crashed on to the table, and pieces flew off in all directions like sparks, all round the room. Some spurted against the mirrors, like hard pebbles, causing the mirrors to crack.

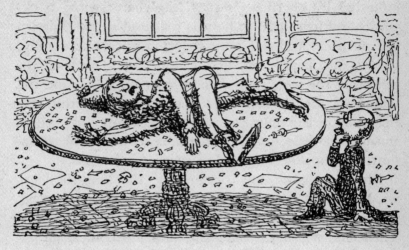

In the vast ensuing silence Arbuthnot could hear a low groaning. He crawled out from under the table. The room was littered with thousands of pieces of glass, like hailstones after a storm. Elsewhere lay on the table, sprawled, inert, his clothes torn and ribboned in many pieces. Across his back was a great gash from which sawdust was bleeding, and his head was hanging half off.

NINE

Dr Solomon Tump was a tall and distinguished-looking elderly man. He looked down kindly at Odd, and then lifted him up on to a high bed. Cheerful-looking nurses brought bowls, syringes, bandages. Dr Tump swung various lamps into position in order to examine Odd more closely.

'Mr Odd,' he said, in a rather high-pitched, scholarly voice, 'you and your friend, Mr Elsewhere, are becoming rather notorious I see.'

'Oh, really?' replied Odd. He had been feeling a little alarmed as he watched all the preparations around him. He had wondered whether they were going to cut him up and, if so, what they would find inside. Now, however, he perked up.

'Yes. Really,' smiled Dr Solomon Tump. 'Nurse! Hand me that evening paper, if you please. The *late* edition. There, you see! All over the centre page!'

Odd looked with amazement at photographs of himself and Elsewhere parachuting across Regent's Park; of Elsewhere somersaulting outside the theatre in St Martin's Lane; and he and Elsewhere riding behind Arbuthnot.

'All London is talking about you,' observed Dr Tump.
'I am sure that when you woke up this morning you
did not expect to find yourself famous by the end of
the day, now did you?'

'Oh, no, sir! Indeed I was feeling rather sorry for
myself and distinctly odd – as opposed to being merely
Odd, you understand?' And he proceeded to tell the
doctor and the nurses the whole story of that day's
many adventures.

One of the nurses made tea, and the matron produced
a tin of chocolate biscuits. There they were, Odd seated
in the centre, on the operating table, all drinking tea
and munching chocolate biscuits, and not minding at
all about the crumbs. They were so busy laughing and
talking that they did not hear the chiming of the
chandelier next door. Odd was so busy telling the

story of his adventures with Elsewhere that he never noticed the doctor sewing-on his arm until, in a moment of excitement, when he was demonstrating how the sandwich-board men had done their dance, he swung up *both* his arms with a cry of, 'Oi!'

And it was at that precise moment that a white-faced nurse entered the room and whispered to the doctor. All at once the laughter stopped. A nurse took Odd away, down to the nurses' parlour, to watch the television, telling him that the doctor would be down shortly.

In the meantime, Elsewhere was wheeled in on a stretcher and lifted at once on to the operating table. Surgeons, wearing white coats and masks over their faces, entered the room. Nurses brought them rubber gloves to put on. Lights were lowered from the ceiling, and all the doctors and surgeons and nurses gathered in a circle about the operating table, to try and piece together the silent form of Elsewhere.

Odd was seated in an armchair, sipping lemonade through three straws and watching a film about a teddy-bears' picnic, when there came a gentle knock at the door.

'Come in!' he said absently, absorbed in the television, and trying not to get his straws too wet and limp by sucking at them too much.

'Oh, hullo, Arbuthnot!' he said. 'Do look. It's a film about three bears who go off on a picnic and then when they come back, they find a strange girl has

been eating out of their dishes, and sleeping in their beds, and sitting on their chairs.'

Arbuthnot decided not to say anything just yet about Elsewhere, so he sat with Odd, watching the television. When the film was over the matron entered the room and spoke quietly to Arbuthnot. He then took Odd by the paw, and as they started to climb the marble stairs behind the matron, he explained to Odd what had happened.

They entered a small room and there lay Elsewhere, covered with bandages from head to foot. Dr Solomon Tump was smiling and saying, 'It's like Humpty Dumpty! Except that, unlike all the King's horses and all the King's men who couldn't put poor Humpty

together again, we have been successful. But he'll have
to stay here for quite a while, until he's recovered from
the shock, and to give the stitches time to settle.'

Odd stood at the end of the bed, looking down at his
friend, lying there all white and silent. He remembered how Elsewhere had fainted in the morning and
been put to bed by Collander Moll. And how Collander
Moll had especially told him, 'Now, Odd, you must
take care of Elsewhere, and don't get into any trouble!'
He blushed brown and felt very guilty, because if
only he had taken Elsewhere in with him to see the
doctor, this would never have happened.

At that moment, between a slit in the bandages, Odd
could see Elsewhere looking at him, and one eye

winked, as though to say – 'Don't you worry about me!' Odd smiled, and reaching out his two arms, one each side of Elsewhere, stooped and kissed the top of the bandages where he imagined his head to be.

'Good night, Elsewhere,' he said. 'I'll be back tomorrow.'

TEN

Every day Odd would visit Elsewhere in hospital, taking small presents: flowers from the garden, a bird's feather, a twig of cones, or some string for a cat's cradle. At first Elsewhere could only lie, listening to Odd's stories, and gazing at the things which Odd held up for him to see. But each day he improved, until by the end of the second week he was able to sit up in bed and move his arms and legs. Odd had found all sorts of different ways of travelling to the hospital. Once he even got a lift on a fire engine and was allowed to wear the fireman's helmet. Another time he travelled on the milkman's cart.

One day he was very late leaving because he had insisted on helping Collander Moll bake a fresh lot of gingerbread-men. He had stuck in currants for eyes and nose, and a piece of peel for the mouth. Moll even made two to resemble Odd and Elsewhere!

'Now off you go!' she said briskly, as she popped the trays into the oven. 'Otherwise you'll be late!'

It was one of those afternoons when everybody seemed to be out of doors and the sun was very hot. Odd stopped to watch the children having donkey

rides on the Heath. He joined the small crowd around the Punch and Judy booth. He watched the kites being flown. Going downhill he stopped to chat with the newspaper lady, the tobacconist, and the lady in the sweet shop. Everybody knew Odd and he knew everybody.

By the time he arrived at the hospital he was very late. It would almost be time for tea – tea and honeyed toast. But when he got to Elsewhere's room it was empty! Thinking perhaps he had gone out for a few minutes, Odd sat on a chair and studied the chart at the end of the bed which showed the rise and fall of Elsewhere's temperature. Far below, in the street, he could hear the honking of cars and the murmur of voices.

His gaze wandered round the room and for the first time he noticed that there was another door into the room, a much smaller one in the far corner. He wondered what it was – perhaps another cupboard, like the one he had found Elsewhere in when they had first met. Suddenly he noticed something sticking out from under the door. He ambled over to see what it was. It was a bandage, one of Elsewhere's! The door was slightly ajar so he pushed it wide open. Now he was in a kind of turret, with a spiral staircase. Up the staircase, round and round, trailed the bandage! Odd began to roll it up into a ball as he climbed up and round, up and round, up and round, until at last he came to a small room. Here he found the bandage tightly knotted to an iron bed and the rest of it stretched taut across the room, and going out through a small window. He wandered over to the window. The noise of people in the street below seemed much louder up here in this empty room. He leaned out of the window and gasped.

'Oh, my!' he murmured. 'Oh, my!'

Down below, the street was packed with cars and people. All the cars were honking their horns, and the drivers looking upwards. The people in the crowd were also looking up and cheering.

'Oh, my!' murmured Odd, gazing down. 'Oh, my!'

For there, halfway down, was Elsewhere, slowly climbing down the bandage!

'Oh, my 'oodness, oh, my Oddness!' he gasped. Then he turned and started to run very quickly down the stairs,

ROUND and ROUND and ROUND and ―

until suddenly he fell

   phlumphety-phlumph,
   phlumphety-phlumph,
   phlumphety-phlumph!

all the way down – until he came out in a room through the open window of which he could see the end of the bandage and Elsewhere already coming into sight.

Odd tugged at the bandage so that suddenly Elsewhere found himself taking a sharp turn back into the building and coming face to face with Odd!

'Oh, my Oddity! What are you up to now?' exclaimed the latter.

Elsewhere, his head bandages slipping, sat on the floor and explained.

'I was so bored, and you didn't come, so I left a note for the nurse under my pillow to say I was much better and had gone home.'

'But suppose you had fallen! Then you would have had to stay in hospital even longer. Couldn't you have

found a simpler way of leaving, in disguise or something? Or in the laundry basket, or – ' Odd paused. He couldn't really think of anything else. 'Now you'll be in the papers again, with all those people out there, and all that noise, and a traffic jam! I think you are a show-off!'

'Of course I am!' laughed Elsewhere. 'I love being in the papers, you know. I'm a Show-Man! You can't be a clown and not be a show-off. You're a Bear and you like Honey. I'm a Clown and I like crowds and people taking notice of me and applauding. That's part of my nature.'

Odd pondered this. 'A bear is a bear is a bear is a bear is a bear!' he said.

'And a clown's a clown for a' that!' replied Elsewhere. 'So bear up!'

And then they both laughed and fell about, pummelling each other, until Elsewhere shouted, 'Be careful, or my stitches will all come out! I'm still an invalid, you know!'

'Ah-ha!' chortled Odd. 'And that is why you ought to go back and wait until Dr Tump says it's all right for you to leave. Besides, I want my tea *and* my toast *and* my honey, and I won't get any if you're missing. So, come on!'

With that he dragged Elsewhere by the arm and they climbed all the way back up the spiral staircase, round and round and round and they got dizzier and dizzier and dizzier –

'But do you know,' exclaimed Elsewhere as they finally got to his room, 'I really am almost better. I mean, that's a lot of exercise in one afternoon for an invalid clown.'

'It'll only be a day or two longer and then – '

'And then?' grinned Elsewhere, looking at his friend.

'We'll do this!' replied Odd.

'And that!' answered Elsewhere.

'And this – and that – and this – and that!'

They began to clap hands, shouting together, laughing, going faster and faster –

'And this and that and this and that and this and that – '

'Tea!' shouted Matron.

'And that's that!' cried Elsewhere.

'Goodness me!' laughed Matron. 'I do declare you are almost better!'

ELEVEN

A few days later Elsewhere finally came out of hospital. He had new legs, made of black and white striped ticking. He wore a new patchwork smock and his hair was now a bright daffodil yellow.

'I think yellow is a gayer colour, don't you?' he said to Odd.

They were sitting on the lower lawn, under the apple trees, having a picnic tea. Elsewhere lay in a deckchair as, officially, he was still an invalid. Dr Solomon Tump, Arbuthnot, and the Matron were seated on rugs. Odd was dispensing tea and cakes.

'Of course,' remarked Elsewhere, 'I once knew a clown who broke his neck doing a double somersault in mid-air and as soon as his neck was mended he was back in the ring doing double somersaults! If you put off doing it you just lose your nerve.'

'But no more chandeliers,' commented Dr Solomon Tump gravely. 'It took us weeks to clean up the mess.'

'And it cost us all the money we made at busking,' added Odd, who had had to pay towards the cost of a new chandelier.

Everyone sat around contentedly, chewing Collander
Moll's sandwiches of wholewheat bread, farmhouse
butter and fresh cucumber. Wasps buzzed among the
jam sandwiches and honey pots; they could hear the
coo-rr, coo-rr! of wood-pigeons – like the soft purring
of a telephone. Hallelujah was mowing the upper lawn
and everywhere was the smell of cut grass.

'I must be getting back soon,' yawned the Matron,
politely placing her hand before her mouth. 'If I stay
here much longer I shan't want to do any work. It's
so quiet and peaceful here.'

'If you care to wait for me,' commented Dr Solomon

Tump, 'I can give you a lift in my car. I must just see Collander Moll and give her some instructions about Elsewhere's medicine. I won't be long.'

In his long, black coat and old-fashioned high wing-collar, carrying a large Gladstone bag, he went along the upper lawn, down the basement steps, and lifted the red dragon, symbol of Wales, which hung on the door for a knocker. Ratatatat! it went, which is the same in Welsh as it is in English.

Seeing the doctor go past, Hallelujah stopped the mowing machine, fumbled inside his old tunic, and bringing out his policeman's whistle gave three loud blasts. At once, high up in the house, a window slid up and Collander Moll leaned out, vigorously shaking a mop. On her head she was wearing a floppy cotton bonnet to keep the dust out of her different wigs.

'What is it, Dad?' she called.

Hallelujah gave one short blast on his whistle which meant – someone at our door. Closing the window, Collander Moll hurried downstairs, putting her mop, brushes and buckets noisily into a cupboard. She tidied her hair – as much as was possible – and opened the door.

'There's sorry I am, Doctor,' she cooed, curtseying. 'Do come in. I hope you've had enough tea. Did you like the Welsh cakes? I made them specially for you.'

'They were delicious!' replied the doctor. 'Indeed, if I might so venture,' he continued in a low voice as though about to impart a great secret, 'I was going to ask you for the recipe.'

'Oh, there's lovely then!' cried Collander Moll, suddenly wiping her hands on her apron for no reason at all. 'There's an honour, look you now! Let me get my glasses and a pencil.'

She fumbled among the pots on the mantelpiece until she had found her father's dusty spectacles which she put on, without stopping to clean them. She sat down by the window and scratched away with the stub of a pencil.

'You know something?' she murmured, peering at the paper. 'My sight's no longer what it used to be in my younger days. I can hardly see to write.'

'If you would allow me,' interrupted Dr Solomon

Tump, opening his black bag which he had put down on the kitchen table. 'I think I may be able to help you. I wonder if you would be so good as to take off your spectacles for a moment? Thank you. Now, if I might just have a look at your eyes. That's right, just look up to the ceiling for a moment.'

He closely examined Collander Moll's coat-button eyes and then, turning away from her so that she could not see what he was doing, carefully dusted Hallelujah's spectacles. Next he produced from his bag a spectacle case. Handing back the spectacles he said, 'I think if you try these on now you should find your sight considerably improved.'

'Oh, there's lovely now!' exclaimed Collander Moll. 'Whatever did you do?'

'I think if you keep the spectacles in this case,' replied the doctor, 'you should have no more trouble with your sight.'

Collander Moll soon finished writing out the recipe, and removing her spectacles carefully put them in their new case, before replacing them in the bowl on the mantelpiece.

Dr Solomon Tump had now taken out of his bag six small bottles, each containing a different coloured liquid, with a label inscribed in his spidery thin handwriting: 'Elsewhere – one teaspoon to be taken twice daily.'

'The patient should have one of these each hour,' he explained. 'Above all, what he needs is a good holiday.

A few days in the country or by the sea would do him the world of good and get some colour back in those cheeks. Is this possible, do you think?'

'Well, he could go up to my auntie's in North Wales,' replied Collander Moll.

'An excellent idea,' replied the doctor. 'A trip to the sea sounds just like the tonic every good doctor ought to prescribe. An apple a day and a day by the sea keeps the doctor away. By the way,' he added, stooping once again to speak confidentially, 'I should let Odd go along with him. They are inseparable and have missed each other a lot. That little bear is not as strong as he looks and it will do him good.' He handed Collander Moll a small round box. 'I should like him to take one of these pills daily for the next few weeks. They're flavoured with honey so he should find it easy to take them. They are vitamins A, B, C and D.' He picked

up his bag. 'And let me know how they get on. Mind they send me a coloured post-card.'

Odd and Elsewhere saw Arbuthnot and the Matron off in Dr Tump's old-fashioned car, and then turned to look at Collander Moll.

'What did the doctor say to you?' asked Elsewhere anxiously.

'He said I'd got second sight, boy bach!' she laughed, tucking her arm under her father's. Then she added, 'He's left enough bottles of medicine for you. It strikes me you are going to turn into a regular little boozer!'

The four of them returned slowly to the lower lawn and began to collect the tea-things.

THE END